LIST OF BEAUTIFUL
WORDS AND PICTURES

LIST OF BEAUTIFUL WORDS AND PICTURES

LISTA WARTA

LIST OF BEAUTIFUL WORDS AND PICTURES

iUniverse books may be ordered through booksellers or by contacting:

iUniverse
1663 Liberty Drive
Bloomington, IN 47403
www.iuniverse.com
1-800-Authors (1-800-288-4677)

ISBN: 978-1-4917-9065-6 (sc)
ISBN: 978-1-4917-9066-3 (e)

Print information available on the last page.

iUniverse rev. date: 03/03/2016

TABLE OF CONTENTS

Chapter One

Framing and its contents, line, colour, object, or another as a whole of things containing together and for this term, we called it picture. It could be a correctly inside or a part of from a whole of or more than it.

Sometimes, it appears like so many *dot dot*, and there is no proper *picture* on a whole of it. For a while, it could be as uncompletely description, because no words to describe it proper, no chance, and it would be closer to completely full inside, even on that side somebody screaming for telling it just looks like a star on sky.

Colourful looking

On that side, guide the eyes to make it real with colour and than thinking for more understanding, there are varying of size and everything inside and hiding. But, someday, somebody would know for what detailing it is as an exactly. So, a part of it might be constructing of good character and or not too, if there are some sides exist to loop it on specifictly. Even there are argue exist, most of it just for information and for growing more. As an image "Line is line only".

Colourful looking covered arounding for section.

Correct it with "Is there exist ten types in a pack of". It might be exist and open the other side for unlucky aspects. If there is open side, another exist for closing side. Colourful looking as an argue life.

As human side looping.

A part of people would giving some period of time to see and break it to its micro containing inside, getting for more information, further inside. Sometimes, there is thing that it would make somebody stay in unhappy sense, standing on one side, than go for a while to search for totally inside.

Even, it would giving more action to construct *the picture* in real till there is meaning exist and no care about sacrificing in it. More showing up for more easy thing.

"Lighting looking as erosion and is it nature".

Human and interaction

On this term, there are aspects that close each other, positive aspect and or negative aspect as knowing usually, but it would giving more *life point* as positive point for elaboration on below.

- *Life information*
- *Life space*
- *Life tools*
- *Life time*
- *Life human senses*

Life space

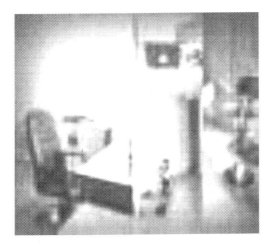

On this term, *life space* is a site of human and interaction. It would giving impact for any activities. *Life space* would growing your interaction as yours. "Growing and added with *life point* inside for *life space* and its term".

Life tools

Life tools and another equipment arounding as a type of things on a whole of inside. On this term, *life tools* are varying of things provided for giving impact as benefit while there are proper tools exist. Call it arrangement books to record, report, etc.

"It could be easier with *life tools*".

Life time

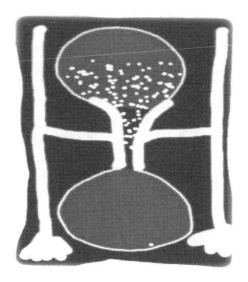

"Flowing as its term and time".

Activities had been finishing finally. For this term, *life time* is the period of activities to finished and there is measuring to showing the period. However, life time as a proper period to showing value.

Life human senses

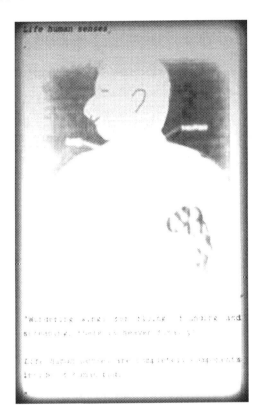

Another line

Happening, there is no time would be exist inside for see, looking for, etc, and for the whole things than "Hoping" as a major, it would be clear next line, without sacrifice *picture*, or there is no more time for another *picture*.

No more action for showing up and it might be stay on face only and than nothing at all.

Correct, *one picture* would mean something inside and it might guiding for another *one* too. It might showing the hiding thing for further too or it might be as tool for completely *picture* too. And it might be happen for a part of people and for a part of *picture* too.

Absolutely, there is *one* thing before go to the next *picture*. For a moment, just stay on with or without any for the only inside as correct thing belong to, it would giving more senses too. For completely feeling, there is *one* thing inside than it would be growing up till it changes overtime. Let it be and flowing.

Another picture

People and another component of it as a part of *picture* and or completely *picture* as the harmonize *picture* and harmonize meaning too. It really in highest level. Another *picture* in harmonize arounding and harmonize people.

"As green colour covering the whole of than growing up".

However

Picture would not have value without something in, that it would giving any impact to another thing.

Let a part of it broked than arrange it as people, people could not explore anything become micro sizing without see any pictures, so, Picture as a part of inside or people as the hightlight inside on a whole of for elaboration to find completely of it. And, no new comer on without any action to see further inside, even, it is about a simple picture. Thinking, if there is no *picture* exist, no see, no reading, no meaning, dark, and nothing exist.

More than it

Let a part of it *lighting* for the correct *picture*, getting more without any missing while it would be on going.

Lighting would be contained with *life point* for sustainability. Growing up and long life exist. Cases, the way of *lighting* does not have *soul* inside than no words would construct the *picture* completely.

More inside

It would closer to growing up the *life point* and let it be as a pack of from varying of types stay together and look at there is *picture* even it would be on

.....*fully* looking
.....*colourful*
.....d*inamic*
etc.

More see

Completely need many chances too. More see and sometimes, there is something added to showing the real character. We called it "*taste*" of picture.

More see and more any as its component in a whole of and it would be as an existing inside.

Chapter Two

In section, looping more, *picture* as a set of object and any such of thing added completely and there is meaning inside too even, it would be hiding as abstract painting.

"Further information for detail, counting and going".

Breakdown for getting major point and detail inside, provided and review on its term. However, *picture* and fitures included organize properly. It is about a set completely which is giving any impacts for another one and changes some part arounding as a whole of components inside.

"Option and accessibilities construct the real object and most satisfy than general item". Statement on line would elaborate it clearly.

Managing exist

"Let some information coming and drop it to some place and putting processor inside than for some reasons, exactly, there is happening inside than there is new comer come up".

It means that it has been showing in real thing and it would be different than before.

It is amazing *picture*, growing and completely. Another side, drop it in some place while managing exist inside and let it on its arrangement, for some reasons, there is happening on side, it appears in good ones on eye and absolutely different *picture* from first. call it product as effect from process working. *Picture* product and planning or *picture* in put, image or mixing all in *one picture* and *product packing*.

Related to statement, the most thing is "Up dated and growing completely as its term".

Look at some pictures below than what kind of pictures exist on it. There is good packing words like "Growed by pictures".

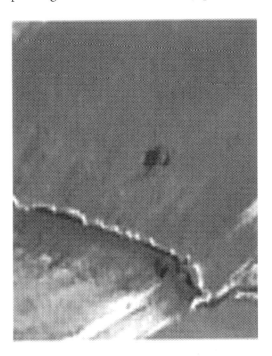

"White, calm, and it looks motion exist regularly". Every body would see picture as usual looking. Even, picture containing varying of components inside. It depend to personal looking on term.

On term, workplace condition is a segmentation site of worker to do their activities and responsibility exist on it. Picture showing us varying of information, especially on condition totally. In fact, there are activities on it.

Even, picture showed on greying. But, it could provide information on some part of it.

"Colour as good thing and even without it too".

Picture showed on greying. But, it could provide information on some part of it.

"Colour as good thing and even without it too".

And look at the picture on below.

"Shading and looking more than before".

Start from an easy thing is usual information on some part of people. It would related to picture which is over old new arounding closer to shading from before. An easy at beginning looking shading next.

"Growing up, giving a different thing on eyes as a part of from a whole of, it is good".

"Supporting totally as the most quote forever and ever lasting".

More see

"Listing every such of and getting the effect, it would be exist".

And than "Powerful and the hiding than showed on side as an independent thing, it looks a wonderful view too". As included on picture.

CHAPTER THREE

Eyes and elaboration

Currently, most of analysis need more than some components containing inside. It would not stay on easy going *picture*. But, a whole of components as correct shaping.

"Eyes is a major and or a segment from varying inside".

As fact, picture would share information as its real. More than it, eyes shared information before, than guiding it for getting picture. For this term, eyes, picture and analysis are components completely for correct shaping.

Ignore a part of from a whole of would guiding to uncompletely, it would grow to proper requirements. Assesment and exist segmentation on comparing for correct shaping on picture arounding.

"If there is missing exist, it just guiding to a part from section *picture* finally".

"Fully and looking showing time, growing up as varying of words containing inside".

LOOPING MORE

"Completely looking might be a kind of resolution on complecated term".

And

"Even there are some types of seasons exist and another still going on too".

Provide it

"A whole of content and its design is just like a first impression than going next".

Than

"Fully and on site, provide it as harmonize thing".

"From senses to effect and it might cover a whole of too".

And

"Even there are some types of seasons exist and another still going on too".

"A whole of content and its design is just like a first impression than going next". Search on picture.

"It had been done and impacting more".

Just share on picture below. It was a history and still exist.

"A bit bright showed on a whole and showing up".

CHAPTER FOUR

Dimention and picture

"Summer time here and pinky time over there and etc.".

Picture: Dimention thinking

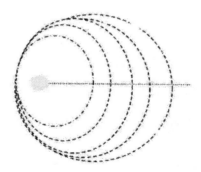

Every such of it is looking like destiny and its term. There is a kind of motor to change the term and it changed as its time. The existence of dimention might be as usual *picture* on some part of sides.

Nearly, it really the most thing for proper *picture*.

"Open the window and there is exist dimention and it would be different".

Let all of it constract the *picture* together and impacted each other. On term, growing the understanding by every such of points on below.

- Time
- Site
- Senses
- Colour
- Etc.

Time

"Action on term with or without any containing for proper".

On section, time would measuring a pack of action as happening arrangement on date. It would working actual over a whole. But, the segmentation is available as commitment.

Segmentation correlated with the separation of horizon. There is actual happen exist on site and it would not totally same on other. While providing many things on tern, it would face some aspects arounding. On case, every such of action would connected each other, even, a simple *picture*.

As a part of understanding, there is principle exist. Let give it more information for proper *picture*. "Operate it as its standard". There is standard operation exist and it would work well. If there is missing in it, it would not giving benefit, over the time. It closer to principle case on term.

"A bit thing could be looking as different case".

Growing more

Site

Look at picture on segment before. It would help for see the hiding points.

"No action well without existence of some part of components as its term completely".

Breakdown it for detail. There are correlation on term.

- Major content as material
- Period of time
- Media interaction
- Managing exist
- Etc.

Major content as information

Capacity of content is domain on term.

Major content would provided and it would interact each other as a whole of *picture.*

"It covered and impacting too. Major but not the only thing".

Period of time

On term, period of time as the result of measuring and showed currenly. Every such of thing would more useful with it.

As momentum showed on the term.

"It would called history on it".

Picture and period of time would giving value and closer to proper thing. There are some aspects around of for identification than going to proper *picture* as elaboration before. Thinking for more, if no existing on actual picture, it looks like shadow.

Media interaction

"Completely success on completely components inside and work as the term".

Media interaction as *pipe* on operation. It giving more benefit to make it easier. For this term, media interaction as aid for completely *picture*. Shared it by eye, glasses and other than exist a whole of *picture*.

Managing exist

"Picture and good looking is an amazing thing".

On looping, managing exist is a kind of good looking on eyes as result from a whole of. Provide it with some part of enjoy components. Every such of it would covering from out side and there is harmonize looking finally than it really looks like managing exist.

Senses

Human and senses as a pack of inside.

Even, there are many sides exist and it would growing for more, it depend to somebody and their *eyes* on *picture*. A whole of feeling using inside directly. As a harmonize inside defenitely on it.

"Even many action done, it would be nothing on comparing with a *completely picture* on time".

Colour

Actual life would showing varying of points on colour arounding too.

"More colour and more preferences".

Information and around of it is just like paper and pen on term. Paper as a space on and give it more value. As informed that the existence of paper just for filled it with letter, etc.

Develop it, every time of life is full of action even, called it a *destiny*. Picture and the varying of colour inside as a complecated thing than let it go to be completely. As for long time exist to see the *colour* of *picture*. More enjoy, for a while everything could be a bit thing too.

"Colouring the term even, it would be nothing finally".

CHAPTER FIVE

Space and picture

"Creating it on its term completely".

Unique field

Specific alarm would inform something to user if there is happening arounding on space and it would related to term. And than, it would rise up for preparing or goes on time.

Space closer to every such of *picture* items position on term.

Every creating have space and it provided on a whole of inside. Look at picture on below to correct it.

Colour

Actual life would showing varying of points on colour arounding too.

"More colour and more preferences".

Information and around of it is just like paper and pen on term. Paper as a space on and give it more value.

As informed that the existance of paper just for filled it with letter, etc.

Develop it, every time of life is full of action even, called it a *destiny*. Picture and the varying of colour inside as a complecated thing than let it go to be completely. As for long time exist to see the *colour* of *picture*. More enjoy, for a while everything could be a bit thing too.

"Colouring the term even, it would be nothing finally".

"Stay on the way is easy for further".

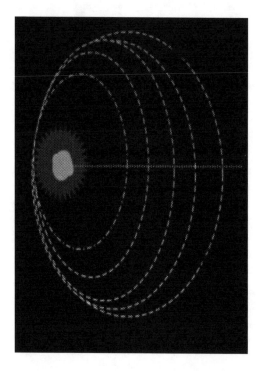

Called it as exclusive conclusion of *picture* on below.

- Life as Resource
- Light as colour
- Object
- Position
- Etc.

Resource

On term, it correlated to what kind of items showed on *picture*.

Light and eyes as a pack of for looping. If the light stay arounding, it develop to another side as chances. More micro components would going out and it changed to more size than exist picture and its unique thing.

"Enjoying the term similar with the existence of colour too". Look at picture on below.

"There are times to showing the correct shape if the times on".

Look at picture and signing on below.

It would guide eyes to site.

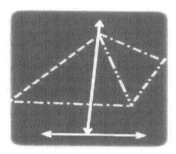

"The signing guide eyes to site, it would more easy on portion. Look at and stay".

"Measuring would showing the case but there is other too".

As showed on picture.

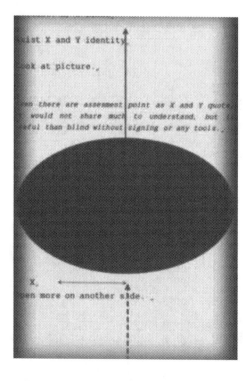

CHAPTER SIX

Colour and *picture*

Colour and *picture* is provided for more enjoying looking and looping further on its correct meaning.

"Drowing and there is exist on eyes".

Identification and exist a pack of picture which are staying varying of aids preferences inside.

It would be showed up stream with looking on eyes, shared more.

"Shade on the line, write it, draw it and without any colour, see next, there are *mode* off".

"More colour and more definitiom and more elaboration for correct term".

"Beginning on bright than finished with dark, cycle exist".

"Even there are varying inside but usual on eyes".

However,

"It would be more colourful on nature".

"Changed and bright on term".

"Similar colour on contemporer term".

"Cover a whole of on colour but stay on a type of colour only than looking around. It might be on mind".

"Stay on mid way while other totally at side".

Provide it on picture.

LIFE POINT SITE

"Lighting looking as erosion and is it nature".

• •
○ ○

"Most of time is just to elaboration than action".

• •
○ ○

"Growing and added with life point inside for life space and its term".

• •
○ ○

"It could be easier with life tools".

"Flowing as its term and time".

"As green colour covering the whole of than growing up".

"Further information for detail, counting and going".

"Option and accessibilities construct the real object and most satisfy than general item".

* *
o o o o o o o o o o o o o o o o o o o o o o o o o o o o o o o o o o o o o o o o o o o o o

"Let some information coming and drop it to some place.

Than putting processor inside.

Than for some reasons, exactly, there is happening inside and impression.

There is new comer come up".

* *
o o o o o o o o o o o o o o o o o o o o o o o o o o o o o o o o o o o o o o o o o o o

"Colour as good thing and even without it too".

* *
o o o o o o o o o o o o o o o o o o o o o o o o o o o o o o o o o o o o o o o o o o o

"Shading and looking more than before".

"Eyes is a major and or a segment from varying inside".

"If there is missing exist, it just guiding to uncompletely picture finally".

"Summer time here and pinky time over there and etc.".

"Open the window and there is exist dimention and it would be different".

. . . .

o o o o o o o o o o o o o o o o o o o o o o o o o o o o o o o o o o o o o o o o o o o o o o o o

"Action on term with or without any containing for proper".

. . . .

o o o o o o o o o o o o o o o o o o o o o o o o o o o o o o o o o o o o o o o o o o o o o o o o

"A bit thing could be looking as different case".

. . . .

o o o o o o o o o o o o o o o o o o o o o o o o o o o o o o o o o o o o o o o o o o o o o o o o

"No action well without existence of some part of components as its term completely".

. . . .

o o o o o o o o o o o o o o o o o o o o o o o o o o o o o o o o o o o o o o o o o o o o o o o o

"Even there are varying inside but usual on eyes".

"Similar colour on contemporer term".

"While on processing and almost over another".

"Words might be segmentation and completely too".

"Space as forever inside. It is a temporal looking on side".

"Correction is looking like losser and hard trip but it would passed away and more easy next".

"Round trip for a whole of to impacting inside".

"On side, the open segment is a fortune day. There are cases exist on up and defenitely on face.

"More than it, looping closer inside, there are empty sides exist. Is it an ambiguation term".

· ·
○○○

"Lost and search as almost happen on life.

Sometimes, for many reasons it would be more impacting each other when there was time exist for looping the losing thing".

· ·
○○○

"Decision is coming from processing and almost of time was not useful finally.

Preparing the time for decision and it looks like nothing for a while, unuseful than down.

But, actually, nothing would be as unuseful, every such of it is space for growing more.

However, it might be staying on it too".

· ·
○○○

"The way of thinking would guide to running a whole of content inside and showed the type's".

* *
o o o o o o o o o o o o o o o o o o o o o o o o o o o o o o o o o o o o o o o o o

"Mature has been staying and tab the site for going on.

But, it might be happening on different condition while there is time exist for sharing".

* *
o o o o o o o o o o o o o o o o o o o o o o o o o o o o o o o o o o o o o o o o o

"While it extracted, another already measure the site totally".

* *
o o o o o o o o o o o o o o o o o o o o o o o o o o o o o o o o o o o o o o o o o

"Understanding a whole of more enjoying duration of life.

Even, for a bit missing exist, impacted each other than staying there and review".

* *
o o o o o o o o o o o o o o o o o o o o o o o o o o o o o o o o o o o o o o o o o

"Information is the most point on condition".

• •

○○

"Thinking for flight and closer to destination and exist more than it".

• •

○○

"Some points might be the most thing and prepare next as a good point too".

• •

○○

"Look at the case for actual and feel it inside than exist life point as yours viewing".

• •

○○

It would be an picture and other picture".

- -
○○○

"Discussion is media for sharing information and breakdown for more.

But, the opposite might be creating too unpredictability".

- -
○○○

"Easy way and going next for facing future term.

But, no thing happen as wishing on empty space.

Getting closer for more chances as its site".

- -
○○○

"Bright the term and it getting changed next on it".

- -
○○○

"Dinamic showed varying of types on actual, it would be difficult on term.

Prepare the site.

And there are more sites for understanding, fully looking".

• •
○ ○

"Flight segment is focusing on going up fastly.

Almost of time containing with varying of action.

It looks like there is no enought time available on term.

Right now and done as such of content inside.

More than it, do such of you closer to it. The argue exist on dinamic".

• •
○ ○

"Proper design would impacting for easy going on case.

For some aspects, a such of has containing more than it and interaction.

Than An easy thing as on side".

• •
○ ○

"If the existence of the term on breakdown specifically, is it correction finally.

Or the proper already".

• •
○ ○

"Segmentation on its stage.

And

Picture and its meaning too".

• •
○ ○

"Organize every such of for its proper ending.

Indication on case because of there are missing on a whole of, than getting information for further.

It would stay on it. Cases arounding on varying of types too".

• •

○ ○

"Putting a glass of water than it would filled it and same as main site.

It showing an adaptation with site, camouflauge, flowing like water going as its way or there is time for doing and finished.

On sharing, cases informed for getting information completely than going to conclusion.

It would be giving more value than stay on uncorrection totally.

But, temporal signing might be useful too".

• •

○ ○

"The signing guide eyes to site, it would more easy on portion. Look at and stay.

Further, there is no time to thinking of it, cause happen on time.

Going down and ready on site with signing.

● ●

○ ○

"Feeling is coming from a whole of body inside.

Even, sometimes it would differently on condition.

As informed, it connected to unstandard effect.

The most of it is cooling down than showed up".

● ●

○ ○

"Waiting time would giving unique term for some people.

Let the time running in it than it would sharing inside to filled in.

More than it, it would exist on a whole of.

Case, every such of thing might be changed and changes".

● ●

○ ○

"The way of life as an open status on its term.

An action is actual thing on eyes.

Than, is there such of it hiding or lost suddenly.

The miracle would telling moreand it exist on side.

However, everything has chance on it".

"Believing as somebody understanding on a whole of, completely.

It does not exist without filling fully.

AndIt has value and not on general.

Loot at the things on market.

Every such of it would telling the price included.

Than, going next.

On term, open more till eyes as completely thing, fully inside".

"Managing on uncompletely picture.

It showed a whole of and guess next.

A bit matter and ignoring.

Tomorrow as the miracle".

"As i know and as you know, it might be differently.

Now as actual and tomorrow as for understanding completely.

Looping more would impacting inside.

"Going more and catching the chances on specific term".

Writer and created by
Lw